LIBRARIES NI
WITHDRAWN

LAURA OWEN & KORKY PAUL

Winnie

D1424835

Spooky WINNIE

OXFORD
UNIVERSITY PRESS

CONTENTS

WINNIE'S
Time Machine

WINNIE
the Shadowitch

Troublesome
WANDS
53
Spooky
WINNIE
75

WINNIE'S

Time Machine

Winnie looked at her garden, and sighed. 'That flower bed looks like a noodle-doodle salad with added slugs on the side. Still, it'll look better when I've planted this nice lolly-lily plant. And it'll give me fresh lollies to pick all summer long! Now, what can I find for the lolly-lily plant to grow up?'

Winnie stuck her spade into the earth, and was about to dig when,

Crash! Ting! Ping!

'Oh dear, oh no, oh blow!'

'That's Jerry next door,' said Winnie to Wilbur. 'Come on, catman, let's see what he's up to.'

High over the fence leapt Winnie the Witch, and Wilbur scrabbled over after her. They opened Jerry's giant front door,

and—**sploosh!**—out swept Scruff the dog, surfing a frothy warm wave of water.

'What in the witchy world?' began Winnie.

'It's me washing machine, Missus,' said Jerry, squelching through a soggy pile of clothes. 'I was just washing me smalls when me machine started banging.

I couldn't find me hammer, so I gave it a tap with me mallet instead and, well . . . it's broke! I've got nuffink to wear now!'

'I'll do your washing in my machine if you like,' said Winnie. Wilbur put his head in his paws, but,

'Oh, fanks, Missus!' said Jerry.

Winnie had forgotten that Jerry's smalls weren't small at all. Jerry's smalls were huge!

'It only takes three of his great soggy pongy socks to completely fill my little machine,' said Winnie. **Squirt-slosh-churn-rattle-sigh-clunk!** went her washing machine as it worked on the giant socks. 'How am I going to fit all his other clothes into it?' she wondered.

Then Winnie pulled out something from a pocket in Jerry's huge overalls. 'It's Jerry's hammer! No wonder his machine was banging!'

Worse than doing all the washing was hanging it up to dry. Wilbur helped Winnie to heave a giant shirt the size of a sofa cover onto her washing line. The sleeves trailed into the dirt because it was so big, and then—

—the washing line collapsed under the weight.

'Jitterbug juice jelly, the whole blooming lot is dirty again!' said Winnie. 'Jerry!' she shrieked. 'You'll have to put up a new washing line for us!'

Jerry tied a washing line between two tree tops, then Winnie and Wilbur flew up on the broom to peg his pants and socks and hankies and shirts.

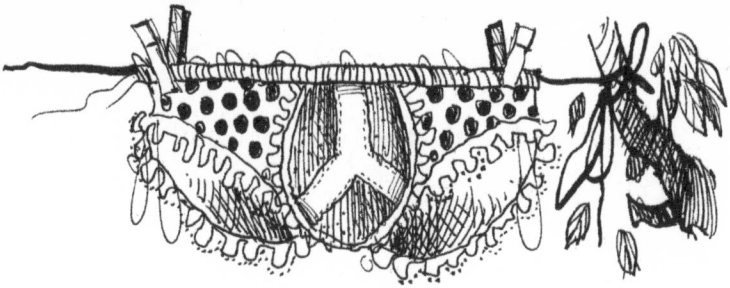

'I never knew you wore such fancy pants!' said Winnie, and Wilbur snickered behind a paw as Jerry blushed as red as a squashed tomato. 'There!' said Winnie, standing back to admire her work. 'All done!'

Flash! Thunder! Rumble!

'Oh, no!' said Winnie. 'Please don't rain!' But it did rain, very hard.

'How's the washing going to get dry now?' said Winnie. 'Poor Jerry's shivering with cold. He needs some clothes, and none of my clothes would fit him, even if he did want to borrow a purple dress.'

Winnie shook rain from her hair. 'Honestly!' said Winnie. 'I've got a machine to wash clothes, a machine to toast toadstool crumpets, machines for just about everything. But what I really need now is a machine to . . .' She was about to say, 'dry the washing', when Wilbur pointed at the clock.

'Meow!' he said. It was time for his favourite *Mice in the Attic* television programme. But the clock made Winnie think of something else.

'Wilbur, you're a genius!' she said. 'That's it! We'll make a machine to turn the time back to *before* Jerry broke his washing machine. Then everything will be hunky-snory!'

They gathered chairs and levers and knobs and buttons, and the clock, of course.

'Stand back!' said Winnie, waving her wand, '*Abracadabra!*'

'Behold a monstrously magnificent marvellous time machine!' announced Winnie. They put on cauldron smash helmets and climbed into the machine.

'Right,' said Winnie. 'Set it for eight o'clock this morning.' Wilbur was just setting the clock when . . .

A flash of lightning made them all jump and Wilbur's clock-setting went a bit haywire.

ZOOM! SHAKE! RATTLE AND ROLL!

They were speeding through time and space.

'W-w-w-where, or w-w-w-when, are we going to, I w-w-w-wonder?' said Winnie, clutching on tight.

'D-d-d-dunno, Missus!' said Jerry.

Bump! They landed in a damp dark cave.

'Ooer-er-er!' said Winnie, her voice echoing. 'Wherever are we-we-we?'

'Meow!' Wilbur pointed to where a fire was burning at the cave entrance. 'Goodee-ee-ee,' said Winnie and her echo. 'There must be somebody here-ere-ere-ere.'

But they couldn't see anybody. Just a drawing on the cave wall.

'Whoever lives here has a cat,' said Winnie. 'And a dog. So they must be ever so friendly!'

'They's got giant h'animals!' said Jerry, picking up some huge bones.

Gulp! went Wilbur, pointing a claw at something, or somebody, in the cave opening.

'Er, I fink it might be time to go, Missus,' said Jerry because the person at the cave entrance didn't look ever so friendly after all. She was holding a spear!

'Oggle-bog-flog!' shouted the cave woman, just as the ground started to shake and a huge hairy mammoth went running by with a whole lot of men and funny-looking cats chasing after it.

'Er, time to go home, and quick!' said Winnie. 'Hold tight!' Winnie waved her wand, 'Abracadabra!'

Whirl-swirl-twirl-clatter.

They landed back in Winnie's kitchen with the rain still splattering the windows.

'Safe and sound!' said Winnie. 'But what was all that clattering?'

'It was them bones,' said Jerry. 'They came back wiv me.'

'Hmm, I wonder what kind of critter they belonged to?' said Winnie. 'Let's see.' Winnie waved her wand, 'Abracadabra!'

And the bones came together in a rather odd-looking way.

'Oh! I don't think five legs and two tails can be right, can it?' said Winnie.

She waved her wand again. 'Abracadabra!'

'That's not right either.'

Another wave. 'Abracadabra! Ooh, it's a mega-mammoth skellington!' said Winnie.

A mammoth skeleton made the perfect clothes rack for drying giant-sized clothes.

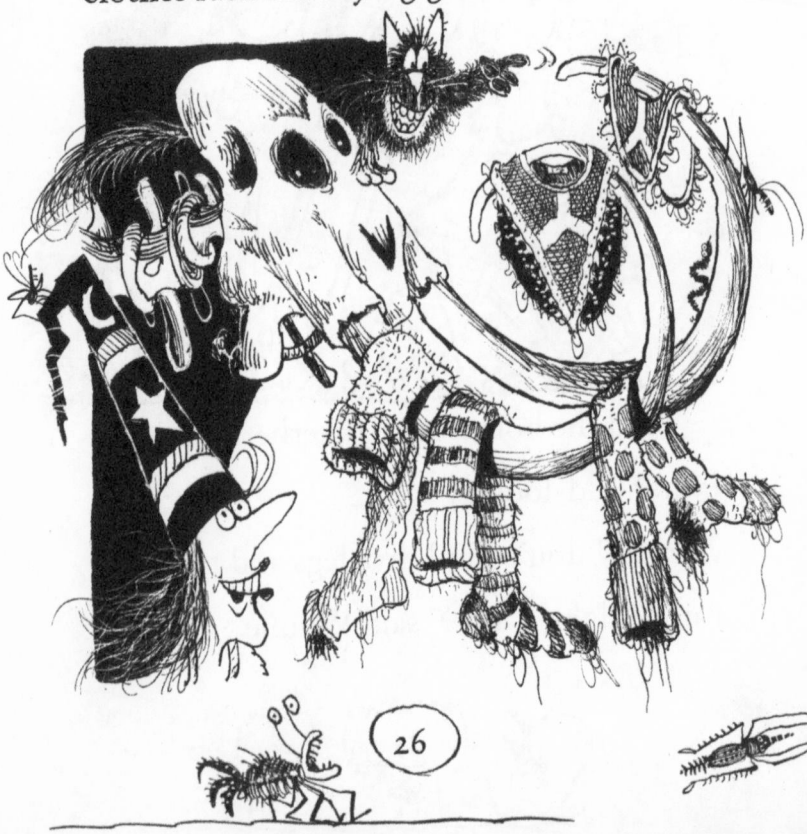

After all that adventure, Winnie planted her lolly-lily, and it turned out that a mammoth skeleton is just what you need for a lolly-lily plant to grow up.

WINNIE
the Shadowitch

One dark evening, Winnie clicked the switch to turn on her lights, but everything stayed dark.

'The power's gone off!' said Winnie. 'We'll have to use Wee Willie Winkie candles until it's on again.'

Winnie and Wilbur weren't sure what they ate for supper. They could hardly see what they were cooking or eating in the flickering candlelight.

'Well, that meal was a culinary mystery tour,' said Winnie, picking bits from between her teeth. 'Now, what shall we do with our evening, Wilbur?' They couldn't watch telly or see well enough to read. But Winnie had another way to share a story with Wilbur. 'I know, I'll tell you a ghost story,' she said.

Wilbur got ready to listen.

'Once upon a time,' began Winnie. She lifted her arms dramatically, and her shadow on the wall suddenly became a huge pouncing shape. Wilbur's fur went up on end. On went Winnie. 'Once upon a time there was a big dark house full of creaks and groans and spiders and rats.

Just like this house, really.' Winnie leant over, and made her voice whispery. 'But the story house was in a wild wood full of whooshy wind and wailing bats. It was as dark as liquorice leeches.'

Wilbur shivered, eyes as big as mushrooms.

'And in this house a cat lived all on his little-old owny-oh,' said Winnie. 'That cat was called Tiddles.'

Wilbur rolled his eyes, but Winnie carried on.

'One dark day, Tiddles heard a **scratch-scritch-scratch.** Just the mice under the floor, thought Tiddles.

But the sound came again. **Scratch-scritch-scratch.** And it wasn't coming from under the floor now. It was coming from above his head. It must be rats in the roof, thought Tiddles. But then the scratching came again, right behind him and louder than ever. **Scratch-scritch-scratch.** Tiddles felt a tap on his shoulder, and he turned and saw . . .'

'**Hiss!**' went Wilbur.

'. . . a ghost! And the ghost said, "So sorry to disturb you, Tiddles my old fruit bat, but I've got this terrible itch in the middle of my back, and I just can't reach the spot however much I scratch. Will you scratch it for me?"'

'Meow!' said Wilbur.

'You're right,' said Winnie. 'It was a silly story. Bedtime now. Up we go.'

But the staircase was dark and dithery in the candlelight.

'Oo, this is spooky!' said Winnie, as she felt her way onto the first step. Her candlelight lurched around the family portraits all the way up. Their eyes seemed to follow her and their mouths seemed to leer and cackle. 'Horrible, aren't they,' whispered Winnie.

By the time they got to the top of the stairs, Winnie's and Wilbur's knees were knocking like a pocket full of eyeball marbles. As they hurried to bed, Winnie said, 'Let's paint some nice new portraits in the morning, and put them up the stairs instead. Nice pictures of us and our friends.'

'Purr!' agreed Wilbur.

So, next morning, Winnie got out paints and paper and easels and overalls, and she took them all outside into the sunshine. 'You paint me, and I'll paint you,' she told Wilbur.

Splash-splat-whoops-splot!

'Er, this doesn't look much like you, Wilbur,' said Winnie. 'Do you mind if it looks a bit, well, a bit, um, "modern"?'

'Mrrow!' said Wilbur when he saw it.

'That bad, eh?' said Winnie. Then she

had a look at the picture Wilbur had just finished. It was a bit of a splatty cat scribble. 'I don't look anything like that . . . do I?' said Winnie. 'This painting lark isn't as easy as it looks. Perhaps . . .' Winnie reached for her wand.

'Meow!' Wilbur had a different idea.

He held up a paw to make Winnie stand absolutely still. Then he put some paper on the ground behind her. Next, he dipped his tail into the pot of beetle-boot black paint, and he carefully ran the end of his tail all around the edge of Winnie's shadow as it lay on the paper. From the tip of her nose, along and up and round and down, in and out and up and down until he got back to her nose again to join up the line.

'Wow, Wilbur!' said Winnie. 'That is one good-looking witch!'

Wilbur coloured it in.

'Well, we've got at least one good picture for the stairs,' said Winnie. 'Now it's my turn to do you.'

Wilbur posed, and Winnie painted around the outline of his shadow on the paper. Then she filled it in with black, all except for two big green eyes and blue triangle ears. Then she added a pink nose and some whiskers.

'Purrr!' said Wilbur when he saw it.

ASHES

They called Jerry and Scruff over from next door.

'There's just time to do Jerry before we stop for lunch,' said Winnie. 'We'll need a whole roll of wallpaper to fit a giant on!'

But, strangely, Jerry's shadow picture came out shorter than Winnie expected.

'Ooer,' said Winnie. 'Jerry's not much bigger than you, Wilbur!'

'Is I?' said Jerry, scratching his head. 'Is I smaller than you, Winnie?'

'Yes!' said Winnie. 'You've shrunk yourself! It must be you doing the magic today Jerry because I haven't touched my wand!'

'So I is small *and* magical!' said Jerry with a giant grin.

As the afternoon went on, Mrs Parmar came to be painted, and some of the little ordinaries, and Winnie's three sisters. 'All my best people!' said Winnie. The strange thing was that Jerry's magic seemed to be working in the opposite direction as afternoon turned to evening. Some of the little ordinaries came out as giants. They liked that!

Mrs Parmar clapped her hands. 'You can tell your science teacher that you've learned all about how shadows are longer in the morning and evening and shorter in the middle of the day!' she said bossily, as she ushered the little ordinaries out of Winnie's garden.

So the truth was that Jerry hadn't actually shrunk himself at all! Which was just as well when it came to hanging the pictures up the side of Winnie's staircase. They needed a proper *giant* giant to do that!

'Brillaramaroodles!' said Winnie, as she looked at the pictures. 'That looks as perfect as a tarantula in a tutu! I shall smile when I go up the stairs now, even if the blooming power goes off again and we need to use wobbly candlelight!'

LETTERS

Troublesome WANDS

Winnie saw herself in the hall mirror, and sighed.

'Just look at that scraggy old hair! Maybe I should put it up today? In a bun? In a croissant? In a doughnut? What do you think, Wilbur?'

Wilbur yawned. Then—**plop!**—something was pushed through the letter flap, which immediately began munching it.

'Oi! Stop eating that, you naughty letter flap!' said Winnie, grabbing the envelope. She pulled out a card with fancy-nancy twiddly-twirly writing on it.

'A witchogram!' said Winnie. The card wiffled with nasty smells and seemed to bubble in her hand.

Luckily for Winnie, who wasn't at all good at reading, witchograms always read themselves out loud in witchy voices.

'Meow?' asked Wilbur, pointing at the RSVP.

'That means "reply soon (to be) very polite",' explained Winnie. 'I'll say "no". I don't like spelling tests.' So Winnie fed the card back to the letter flap. Then she felt in her cardigan pocket for her wand to send her reply witchogram. But her wand wasn't there. It wasn't in her dress pocket or her knickers pocket either. It wasn't *anywhere.*

'I had it just one maggoty minute ago!' wailed Winnie. 'I can't do magic to find the wand without having the wand to do the magic to find that wand that I can't do magic without. Oo, my head hurts!'

'Meow?' suggested Wilbur, pointing a paw above his head.

'Of course!' said Winnie. 'Great Aunt Winifred's wand will be in her trunk in the attic. I'll use that one.'

Winnie and Wilbur went up the grand staircase —**clomp! clomp!**— up the spindly spiral stairs—**clankety clang!** —then up the wobbly rope ladder— **whoops!**—to push open the trap door— **creak!**—and climb up into the dark attic where things squeaked and scuttled.

There was a big musty fusty old trunk in a corner.

'Great Auntie's trunk!' said Winnie. She lifted up the lid—**creak!** Then she plunged a hand into the trunk, and brought out Great Aunt Winifred's . . . best bloomers. **'Euch!'**

Winnie's fingers felt around in the trunk some more and brought out . . .

'Great Auntie's wand!' said Winnie. 'Ooer, it does look a bit old-fashioned, doesn't it. Do you think it still works?'

The wand *did* work, but in an old-fashioned way. When Winnie wanted better light to help her to climb down the wobbly ladder she waved the old wand,

'Abracadabra!'

And instantly there were flickering candle flames all over the attic.

'They'll set the house on fire!' said Winnie. **Puff! Puff!** 'This whacky old wand is just too old-fashioned, Wilbur. I need a modern one.'

So Winnie went to her computer, and—**click! click!**—found Wendel's Wonderful World of Wands where she ordered the Silver Streak 13MXIII wand that had all the very latest features.

Ding dong! Ping pong! Sing a song!

'That's the doorbell,' said Winnie, hurrying downstairs. 'Witchmail is super fast!' She opened the door.

'Miss W. Watch?' asked the postman.

'It's *Witch*, not Watch!' said Winnie. 'Festering figs, do I look like a watch?'

'Well,' said the postman. 'You do have a face and two hands. Ha! Ha!'

'Do you want to be turned into a frog postman?' said Winnie.

'Er,' said the postman. 'No, Miss. Silly of me to say that. Could you please sign here, Miss Whatever-your-name-is?'

'Wow!' said Winnie as she drew the slender silver sparkling wand from the package. 'Look at all those buttons flashing, Wilbur!'

The first button Winnie tried made the wand invisible.

'Where's it gone?' said Winnie.

But then the wand let her know exactly where it was by poking her bottom. It reappeared, and made Winnie jump because it spoke.

'Oo,' said Winnie, licking her lips. 'I would like a big squidgy chocolate puffball filled with onion cream and sprinkled with sugared ants.' She waved the wand. 'Abracadabra!'

But—**plonk!**—it wasn't a chocolate puffball that instantly arrived.

'That would not have been wise,' explained the silver wand. 'I have replaced your order with a healthier option. I hope that you find it acceptable.'

'A carrot! I'm not a rotten rabbit, you know!' said Winnie. 'Humph! I'm going to magic my lovely old scruffy wand back!' She waved the silver wand. 'Abracadabra!'

But the new wand knew better about that wish too.

'Oh no, Mistress,' it hissed. 'No, no, no. You mustn't replace me. Emphatically *no*.'

'But I don't want you!' Winnie threw the wand as far as she could but it just swerved around and came back to her.

She shoved the wand into a drawer and slammed it shut but the drawer slid back open, and the silver wand flew to Winnie again.

'Oh, you can't lose me, Mistress!' said the silvery wand. 'Oh, no, no!'

'Go away!' said Winnie.

'Hiss!' said Wilbur.

'Run for it!' said Winnie.

Winnie and Wilbur fled from the house, slamming the door behind them. Winnie stopped in the garden. 'What are we going to do now?' wailed Winnie, and she clutched at her head in despair. 'Oh, if only I had my . . .' and suddenly Winnie felt something thin and hard and long in her hair, holding it all up. 'My old wand!' Winnie pulled, and her hair tumbled. 'I didn't lose it after all!'

Just then—**crash!**—Winnie's door flung itself open and the silver wand came streaking towards them.

'Help!' said Winnie, holding her dear old wand out as if it was a sword.

Soon she was—**crick! crack!**—crossing wands with the silver wand. Sparks flew, and splinters came off the dear old wand. Then there was a deafening cry.

'Mrroww!' Wilbur ran from the house with Great Aunt Winifred's wand. All three wands battled together until—**crack!**—one of them fell to the ground. Winnie peeped between her fingers. The silver wand had cracked in two. It wasn't fizzing. It wasn't talking.

'Phewy!' said Winnie. 'I'm going to give that silver wand a new job to do. I do hope that it finds it acceptable!'

'Me-he-he!' laughed Wilbur as Winnie pinned her hair back up with a criss-cross of silver sticks.

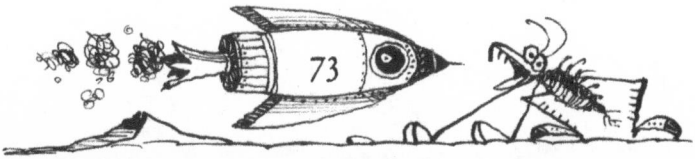

Winnie

Spooky WINNIE

One morning, at the end of October, Mrs Parmar came calling at Winnie's house.

'Winniiee!' yelled the dooryell.

'I have something for you,' said Mrs Parmar, putting an envelope into Winnie's hand. 'The children and I thought it might suit you.'

'What might suit me?' asked Winnie. But Mrs Parmar was already hurrying away.

'Meeow?' asked Wilbur.

'I've no idea at all,' said Winnie. 'Let's open it, and see.'

Winnie pulled out a card that read:

Winnie couldn't read all the words, but the children's pictures on the card helped her to understand.

'Whoopy doop, Wilbur! A Halloween party! We must get ready to go as soon as it gets dark tonight.'

'Let's make some decorations,' said Winnie. She whipped out her wand and waved it. 'Abracadabra!'

Instantly there appeared a flock of flapping black bats. They sorted themselves into a line, held tiny bat hands, and kicked their legs into a jig. Bat bunting!

'Oh, they'll look lovely draped around the school hall,' said Winnie. 'Especially if they give a flutter and squeak every now and again. I must bring some spiders

to make some spooky webs. We can sprinkle the webs with glitter to look pretty.' Winnie reached up to the top of cupboards, and crouched down to look under chairs, and ran her fingers along floorboard cracks, picking up spiders.

'He he! They tickle!' she said. 'Now, let's get Halloween cooking!'

Winnie and Wilbur looked at recipes, then they looked in the larder, and in the garden, and in the bin, and they collected ingredients. They chopped and chiselled and popped and topped and raked and baked. They made devilled gherkin ghastlies drizzled with real drizzle and dusted with real dust.

Slurp! Wilbur licked his lips.

'They do look scrummy, don't they!' said Winnie.

Outside it was getting dark. The moon was shining. So were the stars.

'A perfect Halloween!' said Winnie.

'**Winniiee!**' yelled her dooryell again.

'Who ever can that be?' wondered Winnie.

'Oh, I should have said "what" ever instead of "who" ever!' said Winnie, because, there, on her doorstep, stood a little-ordinary devil and a little-ordinary ghoul.

'Trick or treat?' shouted the devil and the ghoul together, and they held out a pumpkin bucket that was already half full of sweets.

'I can choose, can I? Oh, goody goose pimples!' said Winnie. 'Hmm. Well, I think I'll do a trick then, thank you.' Winnie waved her wand then pointed it at the little-ordinary devil and the little-ordinary ghoul, and she shouted, *'Abracadabra!'*

And, instantly, there were two little toads, sitting on her doorstep. 'Will that do?' asked Winnie.

'Croak! Croak!' said the ex-devil and the ex-ghoul. Fat toady tears began to fall down their warty green cheeks.

'Oh, dear!' said Winnie. 'Was that the wrong sort of trick for you? Do you want me to try something else?'

'Meow.' Wilbur whisper-explained to Winnie.

'Really?' said Winnie. 'Are you sure? *They* wanted to do a trick on *me*, did they? But wouldn't they like to stay as toads for the party?'

'Meeow!' Wilbur shook his head.

'All right, keep your fur on! I'll do it!' Winnie waved her wand again. 'Abracadabra!'

Instantly the devil and the ghoul reappeared, running away as fast as they could.

'See?' said Winnie. 'They didn't want to do anything to me after all. Now what about my Halloween costume? It needs to be spooky and it must go with having a black cat, because you're coming to the party too, Wilbur. Any ideas?'

Winnie got out her dressing-up box. 'I've been told that I'm batty,' she said, 'so how about a bat costume?'

The bat suit was far too small and far too tight. 'I'm squeezed as tight as toothpaste in a tube! This is no blooming good!'

So Winnie and Wilbur threw on a couple of sheets, and tried being ghosts.

Trip-bang! 'I can't see where I'm going,' said Winnie, 'and I can't see to take food from a plate. Being a ghost is no good at all!' They threw off their sheets.

'Oh, if only there was something spooky that really suited a lady and a black cat!'

'Meow?' suggested Wilbur, holding up a

loo roll.

'The Egyptian-mummy look.' said Winnie. 'Great! Wrap me up, Wilbur!'

Wilbur wound loo roll round and round Winnie.

'Ooo, Wilbur!' said Winnie, her voice muffled by loo paper. 'I can't move!'

So Wilbur pulled off the loo roll,

making Winnie spin like a top. 'Oh dear, I don't know what else I can try!' said dizzy Winnie.

'**Winniiee!**' yelled her dooryell *again.*

This time a little-ordinary skeleton and a little-ordinary ghost stood on the doorstep.

'Boo!' said the little ghost.

'Boo who?' said Winnie.

'Don't cry!' said the little ghost.

'Oh, very funny!' said Winnie. 'Are you going to the party? Can we come with you?'

So Winnie and Wilbur went to the party dressed as plain old Winnie and plain old Wilbur, taking their food and decorations with them.

PIN THE CAT ON THE BROOMSTICK
Helen
Laura
Korky
Winnie
Molly
Kate

'Come in, come in!' said Mrs Pumpkin Parmar when they got to the school. 'Come and join in the fun.'

There was apple bobbing.

And pin the cat on the broomstick.

'Mrrrow!' said Wilbur.

There was dancing to the Bony Band of Skeletons.

'Don't stand still, Mrs Parmar!' said Winnie. 'My spiders are making webs on anything that stays still for a single maggoty-moment! Dance to keep them off you!'

So even Mrs Parmar joined in with the dancing. Winnie and Wilbur went wild.

It was a hauntingly-horribly-happy Halloween party. And it ended with prizes for the best costumes, awarded by the headmaster. There were prizes for the best pumpkin, the best ghost, the best ghoul, the best skeleton, and the best witch.

'Your costume was quite a good effort,' the headmaster told Winnie. 'But not as good as this little witch, I'm afraid.' And he gave the prize to a little-ordinary witch.

'Humph!' said Winnie.

But then she found that her gherkin ghastlies hadn't all been eaten at the party. So she and Wilbur went home happily chomping ghastlies and spotting spooks as they walked home through the Halloween night.

Enjoy more magic moments with
Winnie AND Wilbur
KORKY